To Helen Daley, my mom, who's made
every Christmas unforgettable.
–D.D.M.

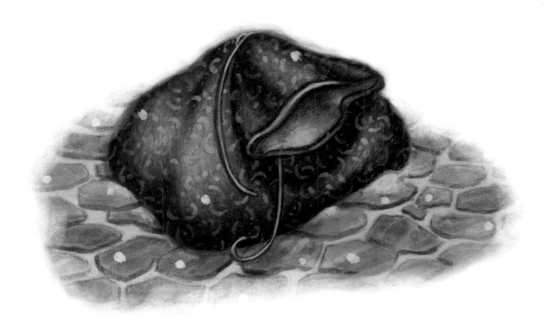

The Legend of
ST. NICHOLAS

A Story of Christmas Giving

DANDI DALEY MACKALL

ILLUSTRATED BY GUY PORFIRIO

zonderkidz
The children's group
of Zondervan

www.zonderkidz.com

ZONDERVAN.com/
AUTHORTRACKER
follow your favorite authors

Nick followed his dad through the snow-dusted parking lot. "Not my idea of fun," he muttered.

"Hey, you're the one who waited until the last minute to buy Christmas gifts for your little brothers," Dad reminded him.

"True," Nick admitted. Why was it so much easier to think about getting gifts than giving them?

Nick spotted a skinny Santa ringing a bell and collecting for the poor. Dad handed Nick a dollar for Santa's kettle. Nick thought about adding something from his own wallet, but he was hoping to have enough left to get himself a CD.

Once inside the crowded store, Nick smelled hotdogs and popcorn. Scratchy Christmas music blared overhead. He dodged a shopping cart.

"You get your gifts, and I'll see to this list your mother gave me," Dad called, disappearing into the sea of shoppers.

Nick headed for the toy aisle, but a rack of CDs caught his eye. A few minutes later he heard a deep voice saying his name.

The voice belonged to a store Santa. "Santa used to go by the name 'Nick,' or 'Saint Nicholas,'" he heard the Santa say to a group of children in the "Elf Room." Nick remembered waiting for his parents in that room when he was a little kid. "A long, long time ago," the store Santa continued, "in a country far across the sea, a boy named Nicholas was born."

Nick leaned against the doorway and listened.

Nicholas's parents were very rich. They traveled all over the world with their son. When Nicholas was eight, they visited beautiful gardens in the Far East. Nicholas noticed children begging for food.

When Nicholas turned ten, his parents took him to the West. Nicholas couldn't sleep at night because he kept thinking about the longing eyes of the children in the streets, children who had certainly never owned a toy.

On his twelfth birthday, Nicholas and his family journeyed to the North. Nicholas waved to the children playing in the snow. "Why aren't they wearing coats and hats?" he asked.

His parents exchanged sad looks. "They probably don't own coats and hats, Nicholas," his father said.

A few years later, they visited the Holy Land, where baby Jesus had been born that first Christmas. "In this holy place, God gave us the greatest gift ever given," Nicholas's father remarked. "Imagine how much God loves us to give us his only son."

"Three wise kings brought gifts for the Christ child to honor and celebrate this amazing gift," Nicholas's mother said, as the church bells rang out.

Not long after they returned home, Nicholas's parents died. Nicholas felt lost and alone. He had plenty of money, but no idea what to do with his life. He looked to his friends for help.

"If I had that much money," said Joseph, "I'd pay all of our bills because my father is out of work."

"I would buy my mother a warm coat," Thomas added.

Phoebe gazed at the stars. "My two sisters want to marry, but we don't have the money that's required from the bride's family. If I had the money, I would give it to my sisters for this dowry." She sighed. "And if I had enough, I would do the same for myself."

Nicholas knew that his friends would never get their wishes … unless …

That night, Nicholas talked things over with God. "Father, could this be the work you have for me?"

As if in answer, the church bells rang. Nicholas remembered what his mother had said about the wise kings bringing gifts to baby Jesus. He thought of what his father said about Jesus being the greatest gift. What better time to give gifts than on Jesus' birthday!

Nicholas could barely hold in his excitement. First, he tromped through falling snow to Joseph's house. He opened a window and tossed in enough gold coins to allow them to buy their own home.

Next, he woke the town tailor and bought his finest coat. Nicholas ran all the way to Thomas's house and stuffed the coat through the open shutters.

Nicholas's last stop was Phoebe's house. He tied coins into three bags for three dowries and searched for an open window. Nicholas was about to give up when he looked to heaven and prayed for God's guidance. That's when he thought of the chimney.

On Christmas Day, Nicholas's friends came running to his house.

"It's a miracle!" Joseph exclaimed. "God must have heard my prayers."

"We were given a gift as well." Thomas began. "My mother hasn't taken off her new coat since she found it this morning."

Phoebe's eyes sparkled like sunlight on snow. "My sisters will marry next month." She smiled at Joseph. "Now I, too, can marry. We don't know who else to thank, so we thank God."

Overcome with joy, Nicholas understood his mission in life. This is how he would celebrate Christmas from now on.

When the story ended, Nick shook himself. A part of him was back with Nicholas. He could imagine how good it must have felt to secretly give his friends what they had wanted most. Nick had almost forgotten why people gave presents at Christmas. He wanted to feel that same joy of giving.

"Nick! Time to go!" Dad walked up, his arms full of shopping bags.

"We can't go yet, Dad!"

Nick never imagined buying gifts could be so much fun. He found just the right toys for his brothers. Then he spent everything he had left on toys for the poor. "I wish I had enough to fill the whole collection box!" he told Dad.

Nick felt sure he'd never look at Christmas the same way. He wanted to remember the gifts of Saint Nicholas, the gifts of the wise kings, and most of all, God's gift of baby Jesus.

There are many legends and traditions connected to our modern "Santa Claus." According to tradition, about 300 years after Christ, a man named Nicholas lived in a seaport town of Myra, in the region we now call Turkey. He is believed to have become the Bishop of Myra and was later called "Saint Nicholas." Nicholas was known as a friend to the poor and helpless.

Every good and perfect gift is from above, coming down from the Father of the heavenly lights, who does not change like shifting shadows.

— James 1:17

The Legend of St. Nicholas
Copyright © 2007 by Dandi Daley Mackall
Illustrations © 2007 by Guy Porfirio

Requests for information should be addressed to:
Zonderkidz, Grand Rapids, Michigan 49530

Library of Congress Cataloging-in-Publication Data

Mackall, Dandi Daley.
   The legend of Saint Nicholas / by Dandi Daley Mackall ; [illustrated
by Guy Porfirio].
      p. cm.
   Summary: As Nick does last-minute Christmas shopping, he sees several Santas
and overhears one retelling the legend of Saint Nicholas, which he takes to heart
as he examines his own attitudes towards gift-giving.
   ISBN-13: 978-0-310-71327-2 (jacketed hardcover : alk. paper)
   ISBN-10: 0-310-71327-7 (jacketed hardcover : alk. paper)
   1. Nicholas, Saint, Bp. of Myra--Juvenile fiction.   [1. Nicholas,
Saint, Bp. of Myra--Fiction. 2. Christmas--Fiction. 3. Generosity
--Fiction.]   I. Porfirio, Guy, ill. II. Title.
   PZ7.M1905Leg 2007
   [Fic]--dc22
                                                        2006015169

Editor: Bruce Nuffer
Art direction: Laura Maitner-Mason

Printed in China

07 08 09 • 5 4 3 2 1